I0836082

First published in Great Britain by
L.R. Price Publications Ltd., 2021.

This edition published by
L.R. Price Publications Ltd.,
27 Old Gloucester Street,
London, WC1N 3AX
www.lrpricepublications.com

Cover Design courtesy of Carolyn Rea Limited licence provided to L.R. Price Publications Ltd for use in this work.

Death's Final Wicket

A.N. Drew

Chapter One

TONY ANDERSON WAS enjoying his week off, watching the England v. Australia second test match at Lord's, in bright August sunshine. The first day had been rained off. *Nothing like the sound of leather on willow,* he mused, contentedly.

Until his work mobile rang.

Always to be carried. Never switched off.

"Come in now," a man's voice said curtly, before ringing off.

Tony got up reluctantly from his seat, took one last glance at the wicket and, with a sigh, headed for the exit.

When Meade rang there were no excuses – no "I'm on holiday," or "I'm busy"; being an officer in his particular branch of M.I.6 meant always being available. Department X was the intellectual branch of the Secret Intelligence Service, known by operatives as "The Brain Brigade". No weapons, just brainpower. Besides, Meade himself never took a day off; he didn't know the meaning of "rest" or "holiday". He had a kingdom to protect.

As Tony drove out of the car park in Gladys, his precious, bright-red 2003 Jaguar S-Type, his mind ran through what the urgency might be. He'd been brought in two or three times before, during rare time off, and the message was always the same three short words: "Come in now."

The traffic was fairly light on this Sunday afternoon, and the lights mainly in his favour. He made good time from St John's Wood to

Vauxhall.

He parked in the underground car park at 85 Albert Embankment, cleared security and made his way to the third floor. Tony was a fit forty-two-year-old, and he never used lifts. His rugged, sun-tanned face, with piercing, blue eyes, made him appear more like an athlete than a scholar turned S.I.S. officer.

"Come in!" rasped the voice, as he knocked on the unmarked door.

Meade was examining a file on his desk as Tony entered, and did not look up. Tony stood expectantly in front of him. After a couple of minutes, the bespectacled, balding head peered at him.

Meade spoke in a deep, matter-of-fact voice: "You're going to Oslo this evening."

Tony waited, knowing that only the bare bones of the operation would be revealed. There was a long pause, while Meade continued to study the file. Eventually, he nodded to a chair in front of the desk. Tony sat down.

Meade spoke in snippets: "Just come in: suspicious death in Oslo. Local police informed our embassy; British national. Biblical scholar; worked at the university. Single. Apparent road accident. You will be collected at the airport by someone from our embassy."

Meade then returned to the file.

Tony knew it was pointless trying to obtain further information – if there was any. He turned for the door.

"Your theological knowledge might be useful," Meade added, without looking up.

Interesting, Tony thought, as he closed the door.

Tony looked over the faces of those holding signs, for passengers arriving at Gardermoen Airport.

And there she was, loitering in the background. Upon catching his eye, Lena Jones made for the exit. Tony followed the attractive brunette at a discreet distance.

He looked at her face as she drove toward central Oslo. He knew from experience that it was a fifty-kilometre drive.

"Been a long time," he mused.

"Sure has: Berlin twenty-twelve."

Tony reflected on their last meeting in Berlin. A messy job, with several embassies involved and international implications: a Russian spy had information, which he wanted to sell to the highest bidder. Tony had negotiated and made the necessary arrangements.

Lena was damned good, he reminded himself now: on the ball and bright. Very bright.

What he didn't know was that she resented him, mainly because they had started a relationship in Berlin, which didn't go anywhere – much to her bitter disappointment.

Her second, slightly lesser grievance was his successful Cambridge background. Lisa had hoped to study politics at Oxford, but had not obtained the necessary grades to get in. This had eaten away at her for all of these years: her having to accept a course outside of Oxbridge. She had gone on to obtain a first-class honours degree, but not from her university of choice. Her grip tightened on the steering wheel, as she relived what she considered to be her two biggest failures in life.

"Right. Berlin." He paused for a moment. "How long have you been in Oslo?"

"Three years. And, you? What have you been up to?"

"Oh, you know, here and there."

"A bit of this and a bit of that?"

"Yeah. Bitty bits."

Lena forced a smile and drove.

"So, what's up here?" Tony always got to the point.

Lena glanced at him. "Something right up your street: religion."

Tony shrugged. He had studied theology at Cambridge, and had looked set for an academic career when Meade crept into his life. Meade wasn't a section head then, but a recruiting officer, who went round top universities talking to aspiring scholars, who might have the talent and ability to benefit the Service. He was persuasive and challenging, and Tony got hooked.

"A British national: Ben Oldham; Old Testament professor at the university. Been here six years. He has an apartment in a residential area. He was killed last night: run down. Local police say suspicious circumstances."

Tony mulled over this information. "Why suspicious?"

"No skid marks; a straight road on the outskirts of the city; good lighting."

"I need to see his apartment. And his study at the university."

Lena glanced over and he caught her intense, dark eyes. "All sorted," she smiled.

Tony leant back in his seat. "Good. So, what's your brief?"

"To assist you – again! Wherever and whatever."

"Okay. It's late; I need some kip. Can you assist with that?"

"We're on our way to the Scandic Vulkan Hotel right now. You're all booked in. I'll collect you at eight tomorrow morning."

"Police first, then his apartment, then the university."

"Of course."

She pulled up outside the hotel shortly.

"Room is booked in the name of James Johnson, the name on your passport."

He smiled, sharing his profile: "Interesting guy. Sales director from Manchester: computers."

"Well, sleep well, James. I'll be waiting in the car in the morning."

Tony got out, stretched and collected his travel bag from the back seat. 'Thanks, Lena. Goodnight."

He closed the door and walked into the hotel.

As she drove off, Lena glanced in the mirror. Again, she saw the white Opel Corsa which had followed them from Gardermoen. It didn't move.

"Bloody yanks! Can't they afford big cars these days?" she smiled, as she turned toward her apartment.

Tony grabbed the television remote, as he fell into bed and pulled up the duvet. As he found the U.K. sports channel his face fell: England were dismissed against Australia in the second test, for a below-par 258.

"Stuff you, Meade," he muttered, and fell asleep.

Chapter Two

IT WAS A clear, cloudy morning, as Tony walked to Lena's car. He had slept well and eaten a hearty Scandinavian breakfast, even trying the pickled herrings from the buffet, with crusty brown bread. The black coffee was superb. He never liked drinking tea on his many trips abroad; somehow, warm water poured over a teabag doesn't hit the spot.

"Morning," she greeted, as he got in.

"Morning, Lena. Cop shop first?"

"Absolutely. Inspector Breivik is waiting for us."

They entered the central police station and were shown into Inspector Breivik's office.

He was a tall, lean, bearded man, dressed in uniform. He came from behind his desk as they entered.

"Mr.... uh... Johnson. Nice to meet you," he said, shaking Tony's hand, firmly. He then turned to Lena and gave her a welcoming nod. "Please sit down," he said, indicating the two seats in front of his desk.

Once they were comfortable, he got straight to business: "Professor Oldham's death is rather a puzzle." His English was almost perfect.

"So it seems, Inspector," Tony agreed. "Please give me the details."

Breivik took a file from atop a neat pile on his desk. "He was found at the side of the road in Sandvika, near his apartment – a popular district with expats. The call went in at 20:26 hours the night before last. The matter was referred to me, as the local police have questions. Good lighting, not late at night and no tyre marks." He looked up from the file at Tony.

"You suspect hit and run?"

"It has all the hallmarks, and the driver didn't stop."

"Any witnesses?"

"Unfortunately, no. He was found by a woman on her way home from visiting a friend. She is a nurse; she realized he was dead straight away, so she rang the police."

"Where's the body now?"

Lisa answered: "In the police mortuary… for special cases."

"For bodies who need a more careful autopsy than normal," Breivik clarified.

"I'd like to see it, please. Do you have the autopsy report yet?"

"Of course. Death was instantaneous. He was hit from behind."

"Cause of death?"

"His back was broken. A severe injury caused spinal shock, and his blood pressure dropped significantly. Anyway, he would have died from loss of blood, with no-one around to call for help."

"Very convenient."

"Very," Breivik agreed. They looked at each other. Tony concluded this was a man who knew his business, and had seen it all before.

"Conclusion?" he asked.

Breivik paused. He had dealt with embassy officials on many occasions, and knew what they were looking for. "Accidental death with question marks."

"Thank you, Inspector. I'd like to see the body first, please, then his apartment, then his office at the university."

"Of course. Miss Jones will take you; she has official clearance. If I can be of further help, Miss Jones will contact me."

They shook hands again, then Tony and Lena left.

Back in her car, Lena asked: "Get what you wanted?"

"For now, yes. But there's more to this than meets the eye."

"The old Anderson intuition, eh?"

He frowned at her. "Not so much of the 'old', if you don't mind! Mortuary, please."

Mortuaries are the same the world over: stainless steel, with gowned figures in white Wellington boots.

Tony and Lena were met by the head man, who didn't shake hands, as his gloves were covered in blood. Above the mask, they saw kindly old eyes and white hair beneath the surgical cap.

"You have seen my report?" he asked them.

"Yes, thanks. Anything to add?"

The pathologist hesitated. "No evidence of drugs or alcohol. Signs of moderate alcohol use; a non-smoker. In quite good health for his age. Everything points to death as the result of a car accident. He was hit from behind. Death was instantaneous."

He nodded to an assistant, who removed the white sheet covering the body. Tony looked carefully, as the pathologist turned the body over, noting the swelling around the spinal area.

"Nothing suspicious?"

"No, everything is consistent with death resulting from blunt trauma, from a vehicle travelling at speed."

"How fast?"

"I estimate the speed at between sixty to eighty kilometres per hour."

Tony turned to Lena. "Do you know the speed limit on that road?"

"Thirty – it's residential."

"Any reports of the speed limit being regularly broken there?"

"None at all," she replied; "it's a quiet bit of road."

Tony thanked the pathologist and they left.

As they walked to the car, Tony pondered this latest information. "Looks like he was a target. But, why?"

"Maybe we'll get a better picture when we've seen his apartment."

"And his office at the university," he reminded.

"On our way," she replied, as they got into the car.

Again, she noted the white Opel Corsa parked a few rows behind. "Our American friends are still with us," she said, as they buckled up.

"Yep," Tony had seen them. "What's their interest? Who's your contact at their embassy?"

Lena groaned. "Dave Brubank. Don't laugh, but he's a real pain in the backside!"

Tony looked at her quizzically, as she started the engine.

"He likes the ladies and comes on heavy," she explained.

"Good. Arrange a meet today – just the two of us. I'll deal with him."

As they drove, Tony looked at the detached, white wooden houses on the hillside. Neat, with large gardens, they overlooked the Oslo fjord. They then passed the blocks of modern apartments, to accommodate the workers of more moderate means. The population of Oslo was only just over 600,000, so they had plenty of space. The entire population of Norway was only about five million, he considered, so there was lots of space in a relatively large, long country. If Norway was spun on its horizontal axis through the capital, the tip of the country would reach down to Italy.

His reflections were interrupted, as Lena pulled up outside an apartment block.

Oldham's apartment was in a modern building. Featuring a lounge, two bedrooms, kitchen and a bathroom, it sat on the second floor. They found the second bedroom was being used as a study. The police had already searched thoroughly, looking for possible next of kin, without success.

As they rolled on latex gloves, Tony said: "You look in these rooms. I want to concentrate on the study."

The rooms were clean, tidy, well-furnished and comfortable – not something which might be expected of a middle-aged bachelor academic. The study was a good-sized room, larger than the one being used as a bedroom. There was a large desk in a corner, with a leather, swivelling office chair behind. The walls were filled with bookshelves, from floor to ceiling.

Tony checked the desk and drawers, and studied the rows of books: academic texts, mainly relating to the Old Testament, with some New Testament works. He pulled out several and scanned the pages.

He stopped at the section of Bibles and ran his finger along them, removing a few to examine their content. One caught his attention: a large King James version. He took it out and flipped through the pages.

In the middle, he found several handwritten sheets of notes, with drawings. He removed them and sat behind the desk. He pushed aside the letters and documents, and laid the notes down.

From his theological academic life, Tony understood the habit of hiding important notes in Bibles. Professor Oldham was no exception. He carefully studied the twelve pages in front of him, frowning.

After fifteen minutes, Lena appeared in the doorway.

"Nothing. He liked espresso, though. Fancy one?"

Tony read on, regardless. Shrugging, she returned to the lounge and sat in the comfortable IKEA armchair, glancing around to make sure she hadn't missed anything.

Twenty minutes later, Tony appeared, folding sheets of lined A4 paper, and putting them in the inside pocket of his smart, navy blazer. She liked the dark-grey slacks, too, with brown suede shoes.

"Okay, let's go. We're done here," Tony said, as he made for the front door.

In the car, Lena waited for his report. It was a while in coming; she had driven for ten minutes and they were nearly at the university.

"Well?" She could contain her curiosity no longer.

"The Holy Grail, no less – that's what he was into."

"Oh," she commented, without enthusiasm, before adding with a hint of sarcasm: "that's nice." She was a good atheist.

"The cup Jesus drank from at the Last Supper? Believed to be the cup Joseph of Arimathea used to collect Jesus's blood at his crucifixion."

Trying to hide her ignorance, Lena said: "Been lost for centuries, right?"

"It was recorded as having been found in Troyes in 1610, but disappeared sometime during the French Revolution."

"So, where does Oldham fit into the picture?"

"Ah, there's the rub: where and how?"

Lena longed for an espresso. "Five minutes for coffee? The uni has a brill café," she enticed, through pursed lips.

"No time. Are we there yet?"

"Just turning in," she replied, hiding her disappointment.

The main campus of the University of Oslo is located at Blindern, a fifteen-minute drive from Sandvika. The university is on four sites, Blindern being the largest, and home to the Faculty of Theology.

Lena introduced them at reception, and they were directed to Professor Oldham's office. News of his death obviously hadn't filtered down to the grassroots staff, as no comments were made when his name was mentioned.

The office was large, with books on every wall.

Tony gestured to the desk. "See if you can get into his computer."

"Easy; the cops gave me his password. Interesting that he had no computer at home. Not even a laptop."

"That's because someone took it," Tony remarked. "Its case was lying behind his desk."

After a thorough search of the office, they found nothing of interest.

Walking out, Lena said: "He would have had about a ten-minute Metro journey here from Sandvika. He didn't drive."

Tony instantly missed his beautiful Gladys, as she flashed across his mind.

"Let's have that espresso now," he commented, as they walked out into the fresh air. "Good cafeteria here, you said?"

Lena smiled as she directed them across the campus.

Chapter Three

LENA DROPPED TONY at the entrance to Frogner Park, introduced him to Dave Brubank and said she was returning to the embassy.

Tony and Brubank strolled around the park, seeming to enjoy the Vigeland statues: eighty acres of Gustav Vigeland's creative genius in granite. As they walked across the hundred-metre bridge, between the main gate and the fountain, they admired one of the most famous statues, "Sinnataggen" or "The Angry Boy": simply a naked toddler throwing a tantrum.

They sat down on a seat overlooking the Monolith. Over forty-six feet high, it comprised 121 figures of all ages, treading on each other to get to the top.

Brubank lit a Camel and inhaled, deeply. He stared at the statue.

"Ain't that just life in all its cruelty? Dawg eat dawg." His drawl was undoubtedly Texan and Tony found it irritating. He had taken an instant dislike to the man. Chalk and cheese came into his mind when they shook hands at the entrance. Who was going to make the opening move?

"Beautiful spot for a game of chess," Tony mused, as he cast his gaze from the statue to the short, moustachioed, arrogant and almost tubby Brubank, in his crumpled, beige suit. He looked older than his forty-eight years.

"Yes, it does rather depict life in all its inglory, doesn't it?"

Silence.

Brubank was the first to break cover: "Guess you're wondering why we've been following you, Tony?"

"It had crossed my mind."

"You've got a sound mind – I'll give you that. Brilliant, by all accounts."

Silence again.

Brubank again: "You're into all this Biblical stuff, I hear? Holy Grail stuff?"

"It has been one of my academic interests. Among others."

"Ah." There was a pause. "The prof was into that, too."

"Was he?"

"Come on! You know he was."

"Do I? How?"

"'Cos you found something in his apartment that we didn't."

"Did I?"

Brubank stared at him. "You sure did, Tony. You sure did."

Tony's face was expressionless in the silence. He thought of poker rather than chess, at this point.

"You show me yours and I'll show you mine, buddy," Brubank smirked. "We can help each other."

"About what, exactly?" Tony studied the figures on the statue.

Brubank lit another Camel from the glow on his last one, and threw the stub on the ground.

"Word has it there's a new terrorist group trying to raise cash by sellin' this Grail thing. Big cash."

"And you think they have it?"

"Nope, not yet. But they're lookin' for it, big time."

"It won't be easy to find."

"That's where you come in, Tone: we need you to find it before they do."

Tony laughed. "Come on! How do you think I can find it when people have been looking for centuries?"

"Where there's a will, there's a way."

"Easily said." He continued carefully: "Just supposing I could find out where it might be, what are you offering to help retrieve it?"

"Cash. Expertise on the spot. The hands to make it happen."

Tony appeared unimpressed. "Sounds pie in the sky to me." He got up and stretched.

"Well, interesting meeting you. And, please stop following me."

"We'll be hearing from you, then?" Brubank asked, though it didn't sound like a question.

"Lovely park, isn't it," Tony answered. "I must come again."

As he walked back toward the bridge, Brubank continued staring at the statue thoughtfully, and lit another Camel.

Suddenly, the naked bodies blurred, then went black, as a narrow blade was slid expertly into his back, piercing his heart.

Tony saw a tram approaching near the entrance and hopped on. It was a short distance from the park to the embassy, and he had a few minutes to reflect on the meeting. He thought perhaps he should ring Meade.

Arriving at the embassy, he gave Lena's name to security at the gate, and within a few minutes she came to collect him.

In her office, he told her about the meeting with Brubank, then rang Meade.

When he had finished explaining developments, Meade was silent for a couple of minutes. He knew his boss was still there, and waited patiently.

"What's your next move?" Meade asked, finally. Without waiting for an answer, he said: "Go it alone; don't get involved with the Americans. Interesting that they're interested. Do you believe them?"

"No. They're up to something, but it's not clear what. Do I have your approval to go wherever I want, with Lena Jones assisting?"

"Yes. You need to keep on top of this one; I have a feeling there's something nasty lurking in the woodpile. Keep me informed."

The line went dead.

Lena looked at Tony. "So, he's happy but not happy?"

"What's new?"

"What do we do now?"

Tony got up from her desk and looked out of the window, as dusk fell. "We go on the 'net and research the Holy Grail. I have an idea where it might have been, but it looks like it isn't there now. There's something else Oldham's notes refer to."

"Oh? What?"

"Codes. There has been research in recent years about a link between possible Bible codes and events in our day. They may be the key."

"Oh, great! Just what I don't want to hear!"

"Come on, grab your coat; I'm starving. Know a good Indian in Oslo?"

"Of course."

"Right. Then we come back and burn the midnight oil, surfing the 'net."

"You certainly know how to treat a girl: dine and burn."

They left the building.

Chapter Four

BACK AT THE embassy, Tony searched on Lena's computer: standard, official-issue Dell. He moved the mouse around the screen, looking at Oldham's notes on the desk in front of him. Lena looked over his shoulder.

"Ah, here we are," Tony exclaimed. "This is what he was researching." He pointed to a series of entries, moving quickly from screen to screen.

"The 'God Code'," he continued. "Never considered this seriously before, but it looks like Oldham did."

"So, why was he killed?" Lena was more than confused.

"Exactly. What did he find that made him a threat? And, to whom?"

"Time for caffeine, I think," she threw over her shoulder, as she moved toward a table in a corner. Removing the water reservoir from the coffee machine, she moved to the door; "Just going to get water."

Tony was lost in thought, as he flicked from screen to screen. He didn't notice Lena's return, even when she made espressos and placed a cup in front of him. "Drink."

"Mmm, in a minute," was his distant reply.

Five minutes later, Lena got up from her armchair, crossed to the desk and held the double espresso in front of Tony's face, with the instruction: "Drink! Now!"

He took the mug and sipped, still staring at the screen.

"I hope you're going to do some explaining soon," she sulked.

"In a minute, in a minute…"

Fifty minutes later, Tony turned toward her, rubbing his neck. “Fascinating. Absolutely fascinating.”

“Good. Perhaps now you will do some explaining? Please.”

Tony put his feet up on a corner of the desk, and gently moved his head from side to side. “I’ll explain on the way to the airport: you’re about to book us on an overnight flight to Buenos Aires.”

Less than an hour later, Lena was driving them to Gardermoen. Their K.L.M. flight would arrive in Buenos Aires at one p.m. local time, the following afternoon.

On the journey to Gardermoen, Tony explained his discoveries so far.

“You probably haven’t heard of the ‘God Code’ or ‘Bible Code’?”

“Correct.” Lena stared impassively at the road ahead, following the beam of the headlights.

He told her what she needed to know, closing his eyes in concentration; the God Code and other publications had become public knowledge. “It’s all on the ‘net.”

“Okay, so where does the Holy Grail fit in?”

“The Bible Code, also known as the ‘Torah Code’, is allegedly a set of secret messages encoded within the Hebrew text of the ‘Torah’. This hidden code has been described as a method by which specific letters from the text can be selected, to reveal an otherwise obscured message.”

“What’s the ‘Torah’?”

“First five books of the Old Testament.”

“Of course it is. Just checking.”

They travelled in silence for a while. Then came the question Tony was waiting for:

“So, how do these encoded messages fit in?”

He was deep in thought and almost mumbled: "Torah, Pentateuch, five books of Moses. God, I need computers – now." Instead, he sat up and said: "The 'Dead Sea Scrolls'. It's in there somewhere."

"Oh, boy, I'm lost. You haven't told me why we're going to Buenos Aires yet."

"Computer programs. Luis Mendez has what we need. He's expecting us."

The 'plane landed on time.

The city was coming out of winter, and temperatures were slowly rising. As they jumped into a taxi they were glad to escape the rain. Tony noticed, as they passed through the arrivals hall, that the outside temperature was only ten degrees Celsius.

Tony looked forward to seeing Mendez. They had met at Cambridge and kept in touch. He knew the Argentine had been doing research for years on the Bible Code, and had developed a series of computer programs on the subject.

The rain had stopped when they got out of the taxi and entered Mendez's high-rise building in downtown Buenos Aires. Tony headed straight for the stairs: eighth floor.

"Can't we take the lift?"

He sighed, with a frown. "Okay, if you must."

Emerging gratefully from the lift, they found a door in a long corridor marked *"Computer Research S.R.L."* The bell was answered by a thin, casually dressed man about Tony's age.

"Hola!!!" The smiling man pulled Tony into his bear-hug.

"Hola, amigo," Tony said, as they embraced. "Long time no see. Can I introduce you to my colleague Lena Jones?"

Mendez embraced Lena equally warmly, in Latin fashion, and led them inside.

Tony immediately looked around the large room, his attention grabbed by big screens on every wall and a bank of technical equipment. “Wow! Impressive.”

“I have the programs you need, Tony.”

“Okay, let’s get started.”

Mendez showed Lena to a seat and they began, moving from keyboard to keyboard, as symbols flashed up on screens. She watched them excitedly scooting their chairs across the floor, working keyboards and pointing at screens.

Two hours later, after numerous espressos, they looked at each other triumphantly from their swivel chairs.

“It’s there, amigo. All there.”

“Yep, sure is.” Tony put several memory sticks into his pocket. Then he reached over to shake his friend’s hand. “We’re staying at the Centuria on Suipacha tonight. Will you join us for dinner? We can catch up on old times. Is eight okay?”

“Si, senor. Perfecto!”

As they left the building, a black Peugeot saloon fired up nearby.

Chapter Five

TONY STARED INTENTLY at Meade, behind his desk. Lena had returned to Oslo.

"We've got a president setting the Middle East on fire, a bunch of Bible codes and a dead American," Meade pondered.

"And a dead professor of Old Testament studies."

Meade nodded. "The prime minister wants answers." He glared across the desk. "So, where are we?"

"Do you want the facts or the version the P.M. wants to hear?"

Meade snorted.

"Oldham was killed because he found something in the texts he was studying, and Brubank was killed because he'd found a connection. A terrorist group is trying to find the Holy Grail, to raise funds. To do what, we don't know. This is all smoke and mirrors; there's something we're not seeing."

"Tell me about the codes."

"The computer programs point to several texts – apparently hidden in the Torah and the Dead Sea Scrolls – allegedly indicating where the Grail might be found. But, more importantly, where the Ark of the Covenant might be."

"Where does that come into it?"

"The Ark is believed to hold the two stone tablets of the Ten Commandments, as well as maybe an original text showing messages intended to predict certain future events. The primary method by which meaningful messages have been extracted is the 'Equidistant Letter Sequence', or 'E.L.S.' To obtain an E.L.S. from a text, choose a starting point, any letter and a skip number; then, beginning at the starting point, select letters from the text at equal spacing, as given by the skip number."

"You're not serious?" Meade stared at him.

"Somebody is kidding somebody. The question is who?"

"For what purpose?"

"Exactly. Two men have died, that we know of."

Silence followed for a while, before Meade asked: "Let me get this straight – to make this code thing work, you need a reliable original text? And that might be in the Ark?"

"Right."

Meade considered if and how he should impart this information to the prime minister. He comforted himself with the thought that it was far too early at this stage – far too early. "Is there any pattern to all this?"

"Not yet. Cast your bread upon the water and see what comes in."

Meade hated anything to do with religion, especially when it threw up scenarios like this. "So, where do we go from here? We're in this now, so we've no choice but to see where it leads."

"Jerusalem is the next move."

Meade tried not to let the thought of mounting expenses cloud his judgement. "You and Jones? To do what?"

"To find out who might be looking for the Grail – that has to be the next stage. We have one lead."

Meade rubbed his eyes, sighing heavily as Tony left.

Gladys purred along the M23, and Tony smiled. He needed to clear his head, and there was no better way than a blast in his old friend.

He stopped at Pease Pottage services, and thought for a while before pulling out his mobile.

It was answered almost immediately.

"Usual place. Forty-five minutes," he said.

"Okay."

Tony saw Dimitri Popov sitting on a bench, smoking his pipe, like some outsize jovial tourist, as he approached The Albert Memorial in Kensington Gardens. Reading a newspaper, he didn't seem to have a care in the world.

Tony sat next to him, and they admired the view.

"If you get any bigger, Pop, you'll need your own bench!"

"And you are far too skinny, my friend. You need feeding up."

"So, feed me."

"Ha! Depends what your hunger is."

"What do you know about a new terrorist organization?"

Popov banged his pipe vigorously on the side of the bench. "There are always new terrorist groups."

"This one wants to find the Holy Grail."

"And I want a big pension and a place in the sun!"

"Have you heard anything?"

Popov pulled out a shabby leather tobacco pouch, and proceeded to fill the gnarled briar, thoughtfully.

"You might try Al As-ka-ri – they are mad enough to do anything for money."

"Based where?"

"Lebanon. Second question?"

"Bible codes."

Popov grimaced; “Why would you ask this of an old atheist?”

“Because it involves us both.”

“Does it?” He lit his pipe and Tony waved the smoke away.

“Who’s using Bible codes to find certain things?”

“Ah, that’s a good question.” He puffed furiously, adding: “The sixty-four-thousand-dollar question.”

“The Americans?”

“There once was a president, of a country far away. A paranoid man. The new Messiah.”

“He thinks.”

“Ah… Well, he might be listening to the wrong people, this Messiah.”

“About what?”

“About how to help him win an election.”

“What’s that got to do with Bible codes?”

“You have studied them, my friend. You can work it out.”

“I need specifics. Which part of the codes is relevant?”

“They claim to have predicted your William Shakespeare. And Hitler. Even the death of Yasser Arafat.”

“Yeah, yeah... And Santa Claus, too.”

“Such a cynic!”

“So, the president is influenced by part or parts of this code. Which ones?”

Popov removed a piece of typed paper from his jacket, looked around and gave it to Tony.

“Where does this fit in, Pop?”

“Use your computer programs.”

“What computer programs?”

Popov smiled. “See you soon,” he said, getting up and stretching in discomfort.

Tony fingered the memory sticks in his pocket, and put the paper with them.

Chapter Six

TONY AND LENA looked about the warm Jerusalem streets as the Mossad officer sped expertly through the Old District, pulling up outside a warehouse in the Jewish Quarter: the city's Mossad H.Q. The driver pointed to a flight of wooden steps, with a door at the top.

The ground floor was dusty and empty, as Tony and Lena made their way toward the staircase.

"Not quite what I was expecting," Lena whispered. "Looks deserted."

"You think?" Tony smiled. "If anyone tried anything here they'd be dead before they hit the floor. Let me do the talking."

They reached the last step.

David Aaronson greeted them at the door, his skullcap contrasting with his prematurely white hair. He was alone. He invited them inside.

"Please sit down." He indicated a long table, with chairs on each side. "Can I get you a drink?" he asked, looking at Tony.

"Water, please."

Aaronson took two bottles of water out of a small fridge by his desk. There were several glasses on the table. He put the bottles on the table in front of them and sat at the head.

"Welcome to Jerusalem. How was your flight?" he asked softly, his slight frame casting a shadow on the oak.

"Good, thanks. Uneventful."

"Good. I am glad. You have come a long way – for what, may I ask?"

Tony stared at him in silence for a moment. Both of their faces were expressionless. He decided to get straight to the point. "The Ark of the Covenant, Colonel. To see the Ark of the Covenant."

The dark-brown eyes did not flicker, nor the pale lips speak for several seconds. "Is that all?"

"Almost."

"So, I call my driver and you go see the Ark. Then what?"

"I look inside."

"If I knew the Ark's location, surely any contents would already have been removed for examination, long ago?"

"Who do you think might be looking for the Holy Grail?"

"What would I know about an old Christian artefact?"

"Whoever finds it finds money. Very useful to a newly formed terrorist organization."

"Yes, it would be – if they had it, or knew where it is."

"Meaning *you* know where it is?"

'Mr. Anderson, you know as well as I do that the Holy Grail was lost centuries ago. If it ever existed."

Tony knew that, in certain theological circles, there is a firm belief that the Israelis know the resting place of the Ark, keeping it secret and well-guarded. "So, you can't help me?"

Aaronson spread his hands. "How can I help you with what I don't know?"

"Well, Colonel, thank you for your time," he said as he stood up, holding out his hand. They shook hands.

"Are you staying long?" Aaronson enquired.

"A few days, perhaps. We want to take in some of the sights before we head back."

"Enjoy your stay. Give my regards to Mr. Meade."

As they walked into the street, Lena commented: "Hell of a way to come for sweet f.a."

"You don't come into Mossad territory without introducing yourself. Tomorrow we get down to what we came here for. Let's get back to the hotel."

"You go; I need to buy a couple of things. I won't be long."

The next morning, they walked a few blocks, spending the time like any other sightseers: browsing the stalls selling spices, ancient artefacts, handmade goods and fresh produce.

Then, Tony hailed a taxi.

"The Wailing Wall, please," he told the driver.

At the Wailing Wall, Tony found a seat in the large plaza in the Jewish quarter, and indicated to Lena to sit down. It was packed with tourists, and cameras clicking everywhere. A man asked Tony to take a picture of him with his family, to which Tony smiled and nodded. He and Lena needed to blend in, to do everything expected of tourists, though he was careful not to have their pictures taken. Video cameras were the most dangerous, sweeping the plaza from a distance, in all directions.

Casually looking around, he approached the Wall holding a piece of paper, and placed it between the gaps in the ancient limestone blocks, without pushing it right in. He then returned to the seat and waited.

Ten minutes later an elderly Jewish man appeared, with a long, white beard, dressed in the traditional black suit and hat. He walked to the Wall and placed his hands on it, his left hand covering the crack where Tony had placed his apparent prayer petition. After much nodding, backward and forward, he was gone.

Twenty minutes later the same man walked again across the plaza, and this time Tony and Lena followed.

He led them through narrow streets, entering an old apartment building. He climbed surprisingly nimbly to the fourth floor, gestured a door, then left. They entered without knocking.

The large main room was a relic from the past, with books and artefacts everywhere about them. As they entered, Rabbi David Ben-Abraham lovingly turned the sacred parchment pages of the Torah, mounted on a wooden platform by the huge windows; white cotton gloves covered his thin hands. He did not look up. Through thick glasses he peered at the text, his worn face shrouded in a greying beard, shoulders stooped in concentration. He could have been any age between seventy and ninety.

They stood for several minutes, waiting. At a nod from Tony, Lena sat down on a once regal leather settee, now cracked and worn.

Tony walked over to stand beside the Rabbi, sunlight gently bathing the script he crouched over. They read the pages together; two Biblical colleagues seeking truth.

The Rabbi then pointed a long index finger at a text, and stood slightly to one side. Tony leant forward intently. After a moment, he stared into the Rabbi's deep, dark eyes.

"There it is!" he exclaimed in modern Hebrew, his eyes returning to the page. He could barely contain himself. "There it is!"

"There it is," the Rabbi replied softly in English, with a gentle nod.

Andrews Air Force Base is located a few miles southeast of Washington, D.C., near the town of Morningside in Prince George's County, Maryland.

That morning, at a discreet house on the outskirts of Morningside, four figures were meeting with the head of the C.I.A. No uniforms, no recording; the meeting never took place. The rest of the house was empty.

In the lounge were the heads of the Army, Navy, Air Force and Marine Corps. Drinking coffee and eating snacks, they might have been at a ball game, but for the grave expressions on their faces.

They were discussing a national emergency with huge international consequences. Such meetings had only taken place three times this century; this was the third. Different location, different faces, but same ominous threat.

The four brass looked expectantly at the C.I.A. chief, who coughed and opened with a firm voice:

"As we all know, the president has gotten caught up in this belief that he is the… Messiah." He paused, looking at their expressions. "Some evangelical pastor has convinced him that it is prophesied in the Bible there will be nuclear war in North Korea."

They looked at each other with a mixture of derision and outrage.

"The president wants to capitalize on this, as an election is coming. If he can be seen to prophesy this war, and doing everything possible to avert it, then he emerges a winner, whatever happens."

"Not if he encourages a nuclear war on that peninsula," the Army general commented. "Says one thing; does another."

"We should terminate the mad motherfucker!" commented Air Force. As he saw their alarmed faces, he quickly corrected: "Not the president! Fat Man Kim!"

"How?" asked Navy.

"Drone. Use a Russian one; make it look like Vlad the Impaler did it."

"Christ!" exclaimed the churchgoing C.I.A. man, without intending blasphemy.

He let their thoughts come into focus. This was delicate territory.

Because, despite Air Force's quick retraction, they all knew what the other was thinking; the general was way ahead of them.

What if the president could be gotten rid of? That was at the back of all of their minds.

It wasn't easy. Security had moved on in leaps and bounds since Dallas in '63. Even with their joint influence, it would be a huge task. But, was it one worth considering?

Army was carefully floating these thoughts, when the C.I.A. chief spoke again. "A curver came in during the night, just to add to our problems: China and North Korea; Beijing has prepared a new deal."

There was an uneasy silence as they tried to sift through this new information. Chinese influence in North Korea was a major issue, but Russia had been networking behind the scenes, and their influence was growing. Fat Man was now being wooed big-time by Beijing, who clearly had a yet unknown agenda. They didn't know if Russia were yet aware of these new developments, but they soon would be.

The China-North Korea border runs for well over a thousand kilometres, from the estuary of the Yalu River in the Korea Bay, in the west, to Russia in the east. North Korea is in the middle of a tasty hamburger.

19th October 1950 is in the history books, but beyond the collective knowledge and lifetimes of all in this room; none were even born. The Chinese People's Volunteer Army crossed the Yalu River to assist the North Koreans, engaging in an offensive against U.S. troops. In effect, the Korean War continues to this day, as a peace treaty was never signed.

The ramifications of this new development were complicated and intense, and could be the catalyst which changed years of diplomacy, with unthinkable consequences. It fitted in with Chinese plans for world domination, and it wasn't going to simply go away. It had to be dealt with.

An expanded alliance between China and North Korea would change the world picture, and send it in a highly unpredictable direction. Russia was reasonably predictable, but China… Hell, they could use Fat Man to…

The worst possible scenarios mushroomed in their minds.

Chapter Seven

TONY WAS SITTING at a table in his hotel room, studying the memory sticks in his laptop. He switched from screen to screen, looking at the page Popov gave him.

He carefully considered the text the Rabbi had shown him. It all came together. The text from the Torah was the final key.

As he stared at the screen, deep in thought, there was a quiet knock on the door. Thinking it was Lena, he answered.

He didn't remember anything else until he woke up…

His eyes slowly started to focus, and he became aware of two men sitting behind a small table. He guessed he had been hit by an anaesthetic spray from an aerosol, as he had opened the door. He shook his head gingerly, as his mind cleared.

Two Arab-looking men stood before him: one casually dressed, in his mid-thirties with a beard; the other about ten years older, clean-shaven and dressed in a suit. They looked at him in silence for several minutes.

The room was very small, like a prison cell. Tony had no idea that he was in a cellar right next to his hotel. He had been assisted there by the two men, looking like nothing other than a typical European who'd had too much to drink.

The older man spoke: "Sorry for the inconvenience, Mr. Anderson. I hope you are now feeling well."

"What the hell did you use?" he asked, abruptly.

"Completely harmless, I assure you. It can be bought readily on the internet."

"That's a comfort," came the sarcastic reply.

"Again, my apology. We wanted a private meeting."

Tony looked around. "Seems private enough."

"To get to the point, Mr. Anderson, you are looking for the same thing that we are looking for."

"Am I?"

"A certain religious artefact."

"There are quite a few lying around in these parts."

"Indeed. This particular item, however, is very difficult to locate. We understand that you can help."

Tony laughed. "And I was beginning to think today can only get better." The two men looked at him without expression.

The elder continued: "It can get better, Mr. Anderson. Much better. There is much at stake."

"And supposing – just supposing – I could locate this artefact, and even wanted to, what's in it for me?"

"Half a million U.S. dollars."

"And, what do I have to do for that sort of money?"

"Use your knowledge to find the Holy Grail."

"If you need funds for your organization, why not rob a bank or two?"

"That would make us common terrorists, Mr. Anderson. With the Grail we would make international headlines."

"Ah, as good guys – well, sort of. I see where you're coming from."

"Then, you will help us?"

"It's a possibility. No more." Then, he added sharply: "I hope you didn't touch my laptop."

"You have my word."

"I'll need time. There are quite a few details to sort out."

"Of course. We will keep in touch. That door will take you into the alley at the back of your hotel."

When Lena knocked on his door, Tony was at work on the laptop. She went to the mini-bar and helped herself to a small bottle of gin and a tonic. "Want anything?"

He shook his head: "Got coffee."

She noticed the size of the large espresso on the table. "What are you up to?"

Tony leant back so she could see. "Been looking at possible sites where the Grail might be. I've narrowed it down to the most likely."

"Where's that?"

"There are many claims about Bible codes. One is that a particular code was written by an extraterrestrial being, who also brought the D.N.A. of the human genetic code to Earth. It is suggested that the alien who brought the code left the key to it in a steel obelisk, which is buried near the Dead Sea."

"That's handy," she said, her voice dripping with sarcasm. "So, we go to the Dead Sea and look for this obelisk, right?"

"Wrong. *I* go. I have the codes needed from the text Rabbi Ben-Abraham showed me: an original Torah text, from the Ark of the Covenant."

"I thought the Ark was lost."

"Don't believe everything Mossad tell you."

Chapter Eight

THE NARROW LIMESTONE tunnel glistened in the L.E.D. floodlights each was carrying, as Tony and the two men from Al As-ka-ri moved forward, cautiously.

The tunnel seemed endless, eerie blackness all around, except for the few metres in front of them. They could just about stand upright, and it was mostly straight, but twisted and turned at certain points. It was also surprisingly warm, considering they were twenty metres from the surface of the Dead Sea.

Suddenly, the lights picked up an opening ahead. They entered a small, bare, circular chamber and looked around, shining the lights on the floor, walls and ceiling. It was empty.

"I thought you said it was here!" complained the older man, his white shirt showing sweat marks under the arms and at the neck. "No steel obelisk. No nothing!"

Tony moved about the confined space, indicating for the men to move to the sides, out of the way. He examined the gaps between the wall and floor, stopping abruptly at two o'clock before him, his light illuminating a crack. He felt the crack to be about fifteen centimetres wide.

"Get the picks," he ordered the younger man, who went back down the tunnel to where they had left them.

Several minutes later, his light shone toward the chamber and he put three pickaxes on the floor: two large and one small archaeologist's axe.

On his knees, Tony chipped carefully into the gap with the archaeological axe. The stone was soft, and he had soon made the gap into a thirty-centimetre hole in the lower wall. He shone his light inside, as the men stood expectantly behind him, their lights aiding closer inspection.

"What do you see?" The older man could not contain his excitement. "Is it there?"

Tony reached in and gingerly felt around, his fingers probing every centimetre. "Nothing."

The older man cursed.

"What the hell! You said it is here!"

"Patience," was the quiet, thoughtful reply. "It is, but not right here."

Tony turned over, to sit with his back against the wall. "Shine your lights over every centimetre, where the wall meets the floor. Look for any slight gaps, however small."

They bent down, slowly and meticulously moving in opposite directions. After several minutes, they met in the middle, and looked in disappointment at Tony.

"Nothing! Nothing, nothing, nothing!" The older man glared angrily at Tony.

"Search again! Hands and knees. Do it!"

They obeyed, wanting to strangle him with their bare hands, but conscious that he was in control – for now. They shuffled off in opposite directions, mumbling Arabic curses under their breath.

Suddenly, the younger man stopped, his light illuminating another crack. "Here?" he pointed, in excitement.

Tony rolled onto his knees and examined the minute crack, barely visible. He chipped and chipped into the rock, making a hole similar to the first. Again, he felt inside, and this time he felt something.

He carefully chipped away, very slowly, using his fingers as much as possible.

With his fingers, he felt a pouch, which felt to be made of some sort of skin. There was something solid inside.

When the hole was big enough, he carefully lifted out what looked like an object wrapped in layers of goatskin, with fur on the outside. As the two men moved forward expectantly, Tony held up his hand. "Wait! Give me light!"

As they both shone their torches his way, he took a penknife from his pocket and gently cut the stitching around the fur. Three sides had been painstakingly stitched with gut, to reveal layers of goatskin. He removed three layers in total, to triumphantly expose a wooden chalice, bearing it gently on the final layer of skin between his hands.

"Behold the cup!" he exclaimed, in all but a whisper.

The men could barely contain themselves as they pushed forward, almost stumbling over each other.

"Careful! Careful!" Tony admonished.

Back on the surface, the younger man got into the pilot's seat and the helicopter took off. The older man clutched the padded freezer bag, as Tony gazed out of the window.

The helicopter landed back at the deserted airfield outside Jerusalem, and they approached the parked car.

Silently, a lone figure stood up from behind the car, as the younger man opened the driver's door.

Two shots were expertly fired from an M.I.6 service pistol, one into each Arab's head. Tony deftly caught the freezer bag from the older man's hands before he fell to the ground.

Chapter Nine

MEADE LOOKED UP from his desk as Tony entered. An unusual event.

"Job well done," he proclaimed.

"I suppose so," Tony replied, as they sat down.

"Come on, man! A new terrorist group has been stopped in its tracks, you've made half a million dollars for our funds, and we've got the Grail."

"If it *is* the Grail. Our experts aren't entirely convinced."

"Well, the Americans are very pleased; big feather in our cap. Not to mention the prime minister. Our branch of the Service is guaranteed – at least for the foreseeable future."

"We need to crack on with the North Korea situation."

"Yes, that's looking volatile. Now Iran has calmed down, North Korea is looking like the next big one; could go either way." He paused and tapped his podgy fingers on the desk, thoughtfully. "Either way…"

"How much do we know about the way the wind's blowing? Any inkling about which way the president will jump?"

"The Americans are being slightly more open now, in view of our recent successful operation; marginally more trusting. But, of course, even they aren't sure which side he's likely to come down on. Changes from day to day. From tweet to tweet."

"So, shall I pursue that angle?"

"Yes."

With that, the meeting was over.

Tony took Gladys for a late-evening spin. He needed to think. The needle touched eighty, then eighty-five, then ninety, as he powered the six-cylinder, tuned 3.5-litre engine, on the M23 towards Brighton. Realizing that he was nudging a ton, he reluctantly eased off. No point in giving the boys in blue a good night.

He pondered the Torah codes, which allegedly hint at North Korea's threat to use nuclear weapons against America, in a terrifying end-of-days scenario. Even more alarming, the codes describe the part that legions of angry angels, the harsh messengers of God, may play in this nightmare scenario.

He muttered to himself as he drove: "The words *'Tsafon Korea'* mean 'North Korea'. *'Aleph'*, *'heh'*, *'resh'* and *'bet'*, arranged sequentially, form the acronym for *'Artzot Habrit'*, meaning 'United States' in Hebrew. Both of these codes are adjacent to the words *'shoah atomit'*, meaning 'atomic holocaust'. On the same grid of Bible codes, the word *'gog'* hints at the possibility that North Korea is the nation which will bring the pre-Messianic war, prophesied to come from the north. Okay, so far so good.

"The name *'Samael'*, the main archangel of death, literally means the 'drug of God', or the 'poison of God'. In the Talmud, *Samael* is described as the angel of death, and commander of a legion of two million angels."

Gladys followed a right-hand curve and the motorway services appeared. He shook his head wearily from side to side, deciding he needed a strong coffee.

"Where the hell are we up to?" the C.I.A. chief asked petulantly, from behind his huge desk.

His deputy, an expert on Chinese intelligence, looked straight at him. "Today he rang Kim offering ten-million dollars, and various contracts guaranteeing prosperity for all. Oh, and a photoshoot."

"Shit! Yesterday he was going to kick his ass right out of the park! What are the White House boys doing?"

"Holding his hand; telling him what he wants to hear; puffing up his ego."

"Business as usual, then."

"Sure is," he sighed.

"Hell, he can't win this election. A well-balanced Democrat president would be one hell of a lot easier to deal with."

"Roger that."

"So far we've managed to keep everything under control. Been touch and go, but we did it. But, this North Korean situation could be the one we can't control. Blue touchpaper gets lit and…"

"Yeah, right."

They stared at each other, as the scenario darkly loomed in their minds.

The C.I.A. deputy chief went on to reveal another bombshell. His Chinese contact had revealed information that, if true, would change the ball game and have international repercussions for a long time to come.

The Ministry of State Security (M.S.S.) had been working overtime. The intelligence, security and secret police agency of the People's Republic of China are responsible for counter-intelligence, foreign intelligence and political security. The logo of the M.S.S. is unique among Chinese government agencies, as it displays the party emblem instead of the state emblem.

Word was that a laboratory in a city called Wuhan was experimenting with a virus, which affected the upper respiratory tract, sinuses, nose and throat, and the lower respiratory tract, windpipe and lungs. His source reported that if this got into the local population, it would spread at an alarming rate to countries outside China, possibly causing a worldwide pandemic. There was no known cure.

"Oh, boy, it just gets better and better," the chief sighed. "Is this a real possibility?"

"Yes, sir, I believe it is. My source says that experiments so far indicate the virus is airborne and extremely virulent."

"And, what's in it for your whistleblower? How reliable are they?"

"She wants to see this stopped before it gets launched. She's a scientist, who understands the international danger if it gets out. As for what's in it for her: her own full research facility here in the States, with enough initial funding for five years."

"You agreed to that?"

"Subject to your approval."

"You got it."

The chief knew he'd have no problem getting official backing; the prognosis was too probable to ignore. A closed congressional committee would consider the cost a small price. And, if the pandemic never happened, funding could always be pulled.

He knew the Chinese were always up to something, and expected some new horror to crawl out of the woodwork at any time. *What* and *when* were the big questions. There was no *if*.

Chapter Ten

MEADE'S OFFICE ON a cloudy afternoon. An update meeting with Tony and Lena.

"So, where are we up to?"

Lena looked at Tony, who was staring straight ahead.

"Well?" Meade was drumming his fingers on the desk.

Tony shifted his gaze, looking straight at him. "We have a problem."

"Tell me about it!" Meant as a cynical exclamation, not an order.

After a long pause, Tony explained the American concerns about North Korea, hanging on the election.

Meade pursed his lips. "So, that's why it's gone very quiet over there?"

"There is one other thing."

Meade's eyes opened even wider.

"Lena has sold us out."

"What?!" Meade's eyes almost popped out. Lena spun to look at him.

"Lena has been working with Al As-ka-ri."

Lena sat up, abruptly. She looked at Meade, imploringly. "What on earth are you talking about? This is complete nonsense!"

"I got suspicious in Oslo, when Brubank was killed. He knew about the Holy Grail. At that point only you and I knew about it."

"Oh, come on. He must have found out about it from the C.I.A.," she countered sharply, still looking at Meade.

"They didn't know about it either, at that stage. We were the only ones."

"That's not much to go on," she said, mockingly.

"Your little meeting in Jerusalem clinched it."

"What little meeting?" she demanded, defiantly.

"After we left the Rabbi's apartment. I went back to the hotel; you went shopping."

"Ah, that. So, going for a walk is a crime now, is it? I don't think so!"

Tony replied, quietly: "Mossad followed you." He paused, inviting an excuse which didn't come.

He continued: "You or someone with you ran down Professor Oldham. And you stabbed Brubank."

Lena jumped up and made for the door. "I'm not staying here to listen to this load of nonsense!" she shouted over her shoulder.

She grabbed the door open, nearly bumping into an M.I.6 officer standing in the doorway. Tony gave him a nod.

Popov puffed peacefully as he waited for Tony.

His bosses weren't happy about North Korea. They wanted a speedy resolution. The situation had been swinging backward and forward; one day there was some sort of solution, the next it was all up in the air again.

Russia does not like uncertainty. All world situations need to be under their control. They are pragmatic and watch all scenarios closely. They keep the lid on when it is in their interest, and cause problems when the lid blows off. North Korea was about to blow big time, with Chinese help. Or, rather, their control.

His instructions were to make waves with other foreign services, to ensure the Americans could not keep the lid on any longer. And, also to discredit the Chinese angle. A controlled nuclear explosion would cause panic in South Korea and across the Pacific. Across Europe, too. The explosion would have to be controlled, but they had the technology to do that – and blame it on China.

The nuclear situation would certainly make waves in the U.S. election, and help to make sure the president was re-elected. Panic demands certainty. Their extensive dirty files were ready to go.

The last thing they wanted was a change of government, with a predictable head who knew what he or she was doing. They treasured what they had in their pocket right now. Literally.

Operatives like Popov were spreading the word across the world, that America was striving to hold North Korea back for political reasons. And, that Chinese influence was threatening world peace. Then, in their time, Kim would be told to blow.

Popov thought about his approach to Tony. He liked him. They spoke the same language, more or less. This was going to be difficult, though; what stable government wanted a nuclear explosion on the Korean Peninsula?

America would automatically retaliate, and Russia could sit back, claim innocence and concentrate on their carefully prepared objectives elsewhere.

"Tony! Lovely to see you!" Popov began, as Tony sat down on their usual bench.

"Hello, Pop. It's gone out."

Popov curiously wondered what these last three words referred to.

Tony nodded: "The pipe."

"Ah, yes." The Russian banged it out and reloaded, making Tony fan the clouds of smoke away.

"So?" Tony spluttered.

"So, my friend, so. All is calm, yes?"

"So… you tell me."

“I love your language. So many different meanings. ‘So’ and ‘sow’, for example. They sound the same, but are very different, depending on the context.”

“So, you brought me here for an English lesson?”

“Of course not. But one does sow what one reaps.”

“So, what are you sowing now? And, what are you hoping to reap?”

Popov smiled jovially. “Touché! I enjoy our little chats so much!”

“Get on with it, Pop.”

“Of course. Well, obviously there is an election coming in the United States. To help the current president, it is being put about that he wishes to contain North Korea, offering lucrative trade deals. Some would say even lining a certain leader’s pocket.”

“History, Pop; old news. What’s the very latest, up-to-date news?”

Popov removed his pipe and stared directly at Tony. “South Korea is being more heavily armed: more missiles; better early warning systems. Supposedly as a deterrent.”

“Well, that makes sense. Maintain the balance.”

“But, how will it help? It is madness.”

“China keeps the North armed; America helps the South. It maintains the status quo. What’s wrong with that?”

“We have been cutting down on aid to the North – drastically. And, I mean *drastically*. So, now the balance is in imbalance. America is arming one side, claiming to be helping to promote peace, while the other side is losing weapons and technical support.”

“Ah, so enter China. Again. You left the door wide open. Still, that could all change with a new American administration.”

“Yes, yes, we hope so. You are right: it could all change very soon.”

“We’ll just have to wait and see.”

“Indeed, my friend; we’ll have to wait and see.”

Job done, Popov put his pipe back in his mouth, struggled to get up and hobbled painfully away.

Chapter Eleven

MEADE WAS IN a worse mood than usual. He glanced at his watch. "I'm seeing the Americans in an hour and the P.M. this afternoon. Bring me up to speed."

Tony told him about his meeting with Popov.

"Conclusion?"

"The Russians are planning to interfere with the U.S. election. Again. And Korea seems to be next on their agenda – along with China."

"The P.M. will love that; he's still recovering from Iran. And Iraq is always a major headache. The good news?"

Tony looked at him in silence.

As Tony steered Gladys toward Lord's, he could not get the Bible codes out of his mind: *Tsafon Korea* means North Korea; *Artzot Habrit* the United States, in Hebrew; *Samael* the angel of death, and commander of a legion of two million angels…

As he stopped at traffic lights, The Monkees' "I'm a Believer" came on the radio. He flinched.

The End.

About The Publisher

Established in 2013 L.R. Price Publications has quickly established itself as one of the leading independent publishing houses in London, truly committed to publishing books by unknown authors.

We use a mix of traditional publishing methods with the latest technology and funding options to bring our authors' words to the wider world.

If you are an author interested in getting your book published, or a book retailer interested in selling our books, please contact us:

L.R. Price Publications Ltd.
27 Old Gloucester Street,
London, WC1N 3AX.

Tel: 020 3051 9572

publishing@lrprice.com

www.lrpricepublications.com

www.ingramcontent.com/pod-product-compliance
Lightning Source LLC
LaVergne TN
LVHW050611100826
845148LV00015B/3218

9781838339579